Bud's Pirate Adventure

Odette Ross

Bud has found a treasure map.

N
X

He sails over the sea.

To a desert island.

But, oh no! A pirate is looking
for the treasure, too!

He chases Bud over the rocks.

And through the caves, until…

Bud pretends to be a sea monster
and scares the pirate away.

Is this the spot?
Bud looks at his map.

x

And

dig,

dig,

dig,

CLUNK!

Bud finds a treasure chest!

And sails home to play.
Have fun, Bud!